This Walker book belongs to:

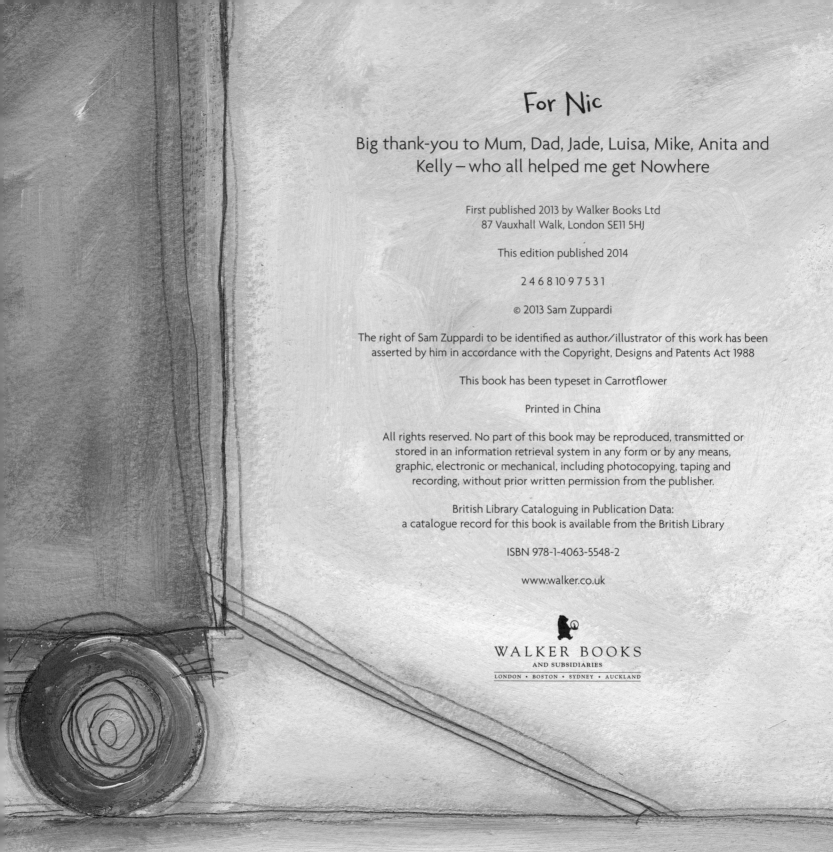

For Nic

Big thank-you to Mum, Dad, Jade, Luisa, Mike, Anita and
Kelly – who all helped me get Nowhere

First published 2013 by Walker Books Ltd
87 Vauxhall Walk, London SE11 5HJ

This edition published 2014

2 4 6 8 10 9 7 5 3 1

This book has been typeset in Carrotflower

Printed in China

British Library Cataloguing in Publication Data:
a catalogue record for this book is available from the British Library

ISBN 978-1-4063-5548-2

www.walker.co.uk

WALKER BOOKS
AND SUBSIDIARIES
LONDON · BOSTON · SYDNEY · AUCKLAND

THE NOWHERE BOX

SAM ZUPPARDI

George's little brother was being
a real nuisance.

So was his even
littler brother.

Everywhere
George went

the littler boys
followed.

George had had enough!

The box from the washing machine was just what George needed.

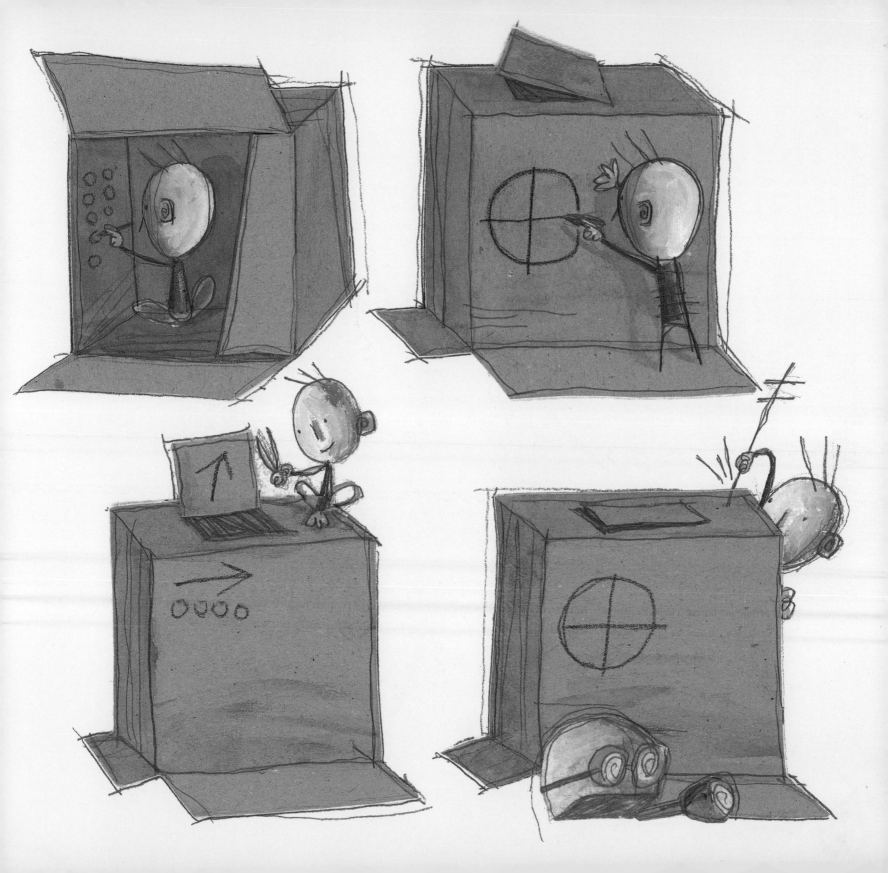

In no time, he was ready for his escape.

George pressed a button...

and
he
was
Nowhere.

Nowhere was vast and empty ...

but not for long.

Soon Nowhere was amazing!

Nowhere was magnificent!

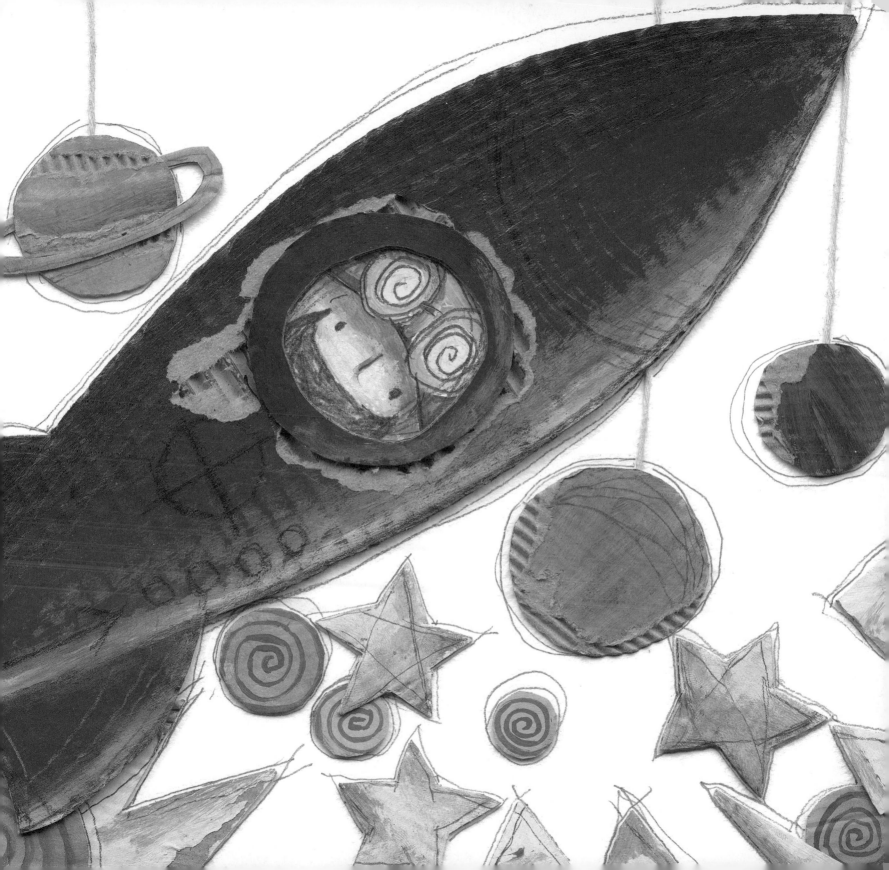

Nowhere was fantastic!

Meanwhile, George's little brothers were wondering where he'd gone.

He wasn't in the bedroom.

He wasn't in the bathroom.

He wasn't in the living room.

Where was George?

He was Nowhere.

But in Nowhere there were no enemy pirates in sight.

And there were no dragons to be found.

In fact, there was no one at all.

And that's when George realized ...

he knew just where to find great
enemy pirates ... and pretty good
dragons, too.

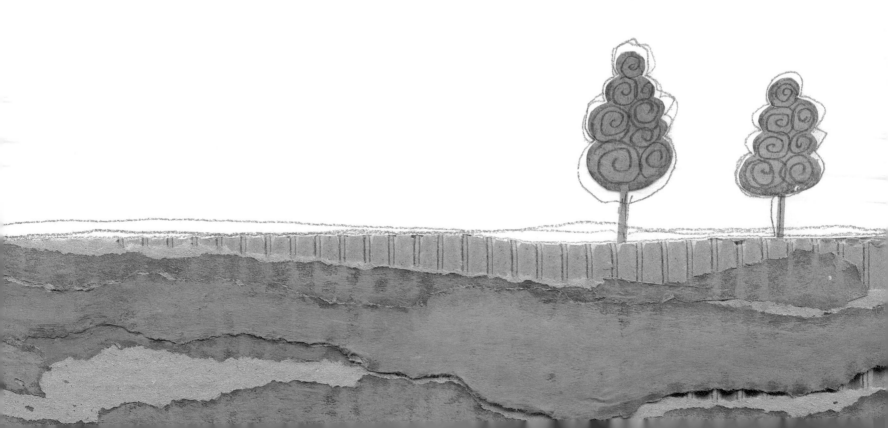

With that thought, he hopped
back in his ship...

and set a course for home.

Sam Zuppardi is a self-taught artist who started off drawing cartoons at school. He has had a number of jobs, including as a bookshop assistant, a nursery worker and a toyshop assistant, and he currently works with children. The Nowhere Box is his first picture book, which he says was inspired by his amazing childhood talent for hide-and-seek. Sam lives in York. He also likes musical chairs.

www.walker.co.uk